KT-454-345

Magic Ballerina
Jade and the Silver Flute

Welcome to the world of Enchantia!

I have always loved to dance. The captivating
music and wonderful stories of ballet are so
inspiring. So come with me and let's follow
Jade on her magical adventures in
Enchantia, where the stories of dance will
take you on a very special journey.

p.s. Turn to the back to learn a special
dance step from me...

Special thanks to
Ann Bryant and
Katie May

First published in Great Britain by HarperCollins *Children's Books* 2010
HarperCollins *Children's Books* is a division of HarperCollins *Publishers* Ltd,
77-85 Fulham Palace Road, Hammersmith, London W6 8JB

The HarperCollins website address is
www.harpercollins.co.uk

1

Text copyright © HarperCollins *Children's Books* 2010
Illustrations by Katie May
Illustrations copyright © HarperCollins *Children's Books* 2010

MAGIC BALLERINA™ and the 'Magic Ballerina' logo are
trademarks of HarperCollins Publishers Ltd.

ISBN: 978 0 00 734877 0

Printed and bound in England by
Clays Ltd, St Ives plc

Conditions of Sale
This book is sold subject to the condition that it shall not, by way of trade
or otherwise, be lent, re-sold, hired out or otherwise circulated without
the publisher's prior written consent in any form of binding or cover other
than that in which it is published and without a similar condition including
this condition being imposed on the subsequent purchaser.

Mixed Sources
Product group from well-managed
forests and other controlled sources
www.fsc.org   Cert no. SW-COC-001806
© 1996 Forest Stewardship Council

FSC is a non-profit international organisation established to promote the
responsible management of the world's forests. Products carrying the FSC
label are independently certified to assure consumers that they come
from forests that are managed to meet the social, economic and
ecological needs of present and future generations.

Find out more about HarperCollins and the environment at
www.harpercollins.co.uk/green

Magic Ballerina™

Jade and the Silver Flute

Darcey Bussell

HarperCollins *Children's Books*

ENCH

Royal Palace

Sugar Plum Fairy's Cottage

The Village

The Land of SWEETS

THEATRE

Theatre

To Phoebe and Zoe, as they are the inspiration behind Magic Ballerina.

Contents

Prologue

*In the soft, pale light, the girl stood
with her head bent and her hands
held lightly in front of her.
There was a moment's silence and then
the first notes of the music began.
For as long as the girl could remember
music had seemed to tell her of
another world – a magical, exciting
world – that lay far, far away.
She always felt if she could just
close her eyes and lose herself,
then she would get there.
Maybe this time. As the music
swirled inside her, she swept
her arms above her head, rose on to
her toes and began to dance…*

The Audition

Jade took a deep breath and let herself go, dancing with all her heart. But even as she moved, she knew she wasn't expressing the music properly. Her feet had too much bounce in them, her wrists had too much flick in them and her arms had too much stretch in them.

She looked up at her ballet teacher, Madame Za-Za. "Sorry, it wasn't really *ballet* dancing, was it?" said Jade, biting her lip.

Madame Za-Za nodded. "You are quite correct, Jade, it was not."

A silence, which seemed to fill every corner of the small studio at Madame Za-Za's School of Ballet, followed her comment. Jade sighed. She'd come to this audition for the end of term show wanting to dance her very best and now she'd messed it up. The solo she'd chosen was one that Beauty did in the ballet of

Beauty and the Beast. She knew the dance was supposed to be smooth and serene and she'd started off well. But then after no time at all, she'd found herself doing what came naturally to her – making it a bit more energetic and free.

A bit more *street*. Street dance had always been Jade's favourite type of dancing until she'd discovered ballet. Now, though, she loved them both.

Madame Za-Za's dark eyes were fixed on her. "You don't always have to jazz everything up to enjoy the dance, you know," she said softly. "You'll find a way."

Jade nodded. "I just couldn't help myself," she said, her eyes coming to rest on her red ballet shoes. Immediately she felt a shiver of excitement run through her that made everything seem all right. It

was always the same
when she looked at
her amazing shoes.
They were magic and
had the power to whisk

her away to Enchantia – a land where the
characters from all the different ballets
lived. Jade had been there twice already
and had the most amazing adventures
with her new friend the White Cat. But
she shouldn't be thinking about that now.
She should be concentrating on her
teacher.

Madame Za-Za was bending gracefully
to get something from her bag – a scarf,

as fine and floaty as a feather. She held it lightly as she talked to Jade. "*Sometimes it is appropriate to bring a lively bouncing energy to a dance*," she said, "but with Beauty's solo, it is definitely not. This is a smooth pure classical solo. It needs soft expressive movements."

Jade knew that everything her teacher was saying was true. She knew the story well and was enchanted by the tale of the handsome and kindly prince who had a terrible curse put on him by a witch – a curse that had turned him into a monstrous-looking beast. And of Beauty,

the girl who had broken it.

Thinking about that now, Jade knew she hadn't got that across in her dancing. How could she have let herself dance so sharply? She was about to ask if she could start again when another pupil knocked on the door and then asked Madame Za-Za to come to the larger dance studio.

"I will be back in a moment, Jade," said Madame Za-Za making for the door. She held the scarf out. "Take this. It will help you give a softer quality to your dance, Jade. See how lightly it shimmers!"

As she let go of the scarf, Jade watched
it float its way gently and slowly to the
ground. By the time Madame Za-Za had
left the room the scarf had settled right
beside Jade's feet.

Bending down to pick it up, she felt a wave of excitement flood through her. Her shoes were glowing! A tingle began in her toes and started to move through her whole body. Jade's eyes lit up as the tingle went down her arms to her fingertips. A cloud of hazy colours began to swirl around her growing more and more bright and vibrant.

Yes, it's really happening, Jade grinned. *It's really happening again. They're taking me to Enchantia!*

A moment later she was lifted off the ground in the swirling, spinning mass of colour.

Missing Items

Jade's feet touched solid ground once more and she stared straight ahead in amazement. Before her stood a grand majestic palace. The sun's rays made its white marble walls gleam brightly and the tall pointed spires glistened

against the blue sky.

It was hard to take her eyes off such a magnificent sight. Jade smiled as she shielded her eyes from the sun with her hand and looked around for her friend, the White Cat. Any moment now he would come bounding up to her. He always did.

"Ah, here he is…" Jade said, but she was mistaken. The person approaching her was a fine upright lady dressed in a long full skirt. *She probably works at the palace*, thought Jade. *Maybe she's a lady-in-waiting*.

"Hello, my dear. What has happened to

your beautiful scarf?"

Jade was surprised that the lady had stopped to talk to her. She'd somehow seemed a bit snooty, walking along with her nose in the air. And it was an even bigger surprise when she began to examine the silver scarf that Jade was still clutching. "Very pretty, my dear. Very pretty indeed. But look, a thread has come loose. Do you see?"

"Sorry? What?" Jade hadn't been paying attention. She'd been looking round wondering where the White Cat had got to. She wasn't all that bothered about a little thread coming loose, but

politely she looked at the scarf. "Oh
yes…" she replied distractedly.

"I can mend it for you."

"No, it's fine, honestly." Jade turned
her head this way and that. Surely the
White Cat would be here very soon.

"No, my dear, I'm afraid it's not fine," the lady started again. "You see, the scarf will unravel completely if left with this loose thread hanging. Let me take it and mend it for you. I can do it very quickly."

"Er…"

"I can bring it back in an hour. Meet me here outside the palace. How does that sound?"

"Oh… OK." Jade really didn't mind one way or the other whether the scarf got mended. All that mattered was that her friend turned up to greet her. "OK, well, thank you very much." And before she knew it, the lady had turned on her

heel and was walking away.

Jade looked round again and this time her heart lurched with happiness as she saw the White Cat bounding along, a big grin on his face.

"Jade! Jade! How lovely to see you again. I hope you haven't been waiting long. I got delayed over a small problem, but no matter now."

Jade hugged her friend and straight away commented on the palace. "It's just the grandest building I've ever seen, White Cat!"

"Then the inside won't disappoint you. Come on, let me show you. I can introduce you to King Tristan and Queen Isabella too."

Jade gasped. "A king and queen?"

"The King and Queen of Enchantia, no less!" grinned the White Cat. "And today their palace is looking particularly spectacular for a very important event!"

Jade nodded trying to take everything in. As they entered the palace she stared around at the high-ceilinged hall and the colourful tapestries adorning the walls. Through a sweeping archway she caught a glimpse of activity. Everyone seemed very busy rushing around. Thankfully the White Cat explained what was going on.

"Preparations are being made for a special ceremony," he started. "A ceremony that takes place at the same

time every year when the First Fairy of
Enchantia arrives to dance to the music of
the Silver Flute."

"The First Fairy of Enchantia?" Jade
breathed. She sounded wonderful.

"The dance makes sure that the baby
birds hatch out from their eggs," the
White Cat continued. "As long as she
dances before sunset, all will be well. But
if she doesn't dance and they don't hatch,
there won't be any new birdsong and so
eventually the music in Enchantia would
die out."

Jade couldn't believe she'd been
brought to Enchantia on such an

important day. Her eyes widened even more as a beautiful lady in a long midnight-blue dress appeared. Beside her was a man wearing dark trousers, a fur-lined cloak and a gold crown.

The White Cat bowed low, so Jade followed suit dropping into a deep curtsy.

Then he began the introduction. "Jade, this is King Tristan and Queen Isabella."

Jade did another curtsy as the King smiled at her and the Queen took her hand. "Welcome to our home," she murmured. "Are you able to attend the ceremony?"

Jade looked at the White Cat who answered respectfully, "It would be an honour, Your Majesty. But first we have some business to attend to, so we will take our leave of you."

"Until this afternoon!" smiled the King.

"Business?" Jade breathed as they stepped outside. "What business do we need to attend to? Oh, I'm so excited – I've never met a king and queen before! Tell me, tell me, where are we going?"

"Questions, questions!" laughed the White Cat, walking briskly as he talked. "We're off to solve a problem – a big problem. You see, things have been going missing in Enchantia. I can only think you've been brought here to help me find them."

"What kind of things?"said Jade.

"Precious things. It's really most annoying." The White Cat pursed his lips. "First Red Riding Hood lost her ruby ring, then the Sugar Plum Fairy mislaid her sparkling tiara. Next Leonardo the toymaker lost his hammer. And now Cinderella is most upset because her baby Pearl's special spoon has gone missing, as well as her own napkin ring. I have an idea who's behind all this, but I'd like to know if you agree."

As they hurried along the White Cat told Jade about a mischievous magpie who'd stolen people's things before. "I think he might be the culprit once again!" he finished off as they approached the tree where the magpie lived.

Jade nodded. It seemed like a fairly safe assumption to make. She crossed her fingers that it *would* turn out to be the magpie, so she and the White Cat could get back to the Royal Palace. She was dying to see the First Fairy.

"Mister Magpie, do you have anything to say?" the White Cat's voice called up the tree.

"I have plenty to say. What would you like to discuss first?" came a cheeky voice from a branch above.

"Come on, Mister Magpie!" the White Cat replied sternly. "I know you've been up to your old tricks, stealing things again."

"I have *not!*" the magpie retorted loudly and indignantly. "For your information, I have been making do with *these!*" A shower of shiny leaves tumbled down from the tree.

Jade grinned at her friend as he called up, "Sorry, Mister Magpie! My mistake!"

"I should think so too! Fancy accusing me of…"

But the White Cat didn't wait to hear any more. "Come on, Jade," he said, "let's go and see if the First Fairy has arrived. We can puzzle about the missing items later."

As soon as Jade entered the Royal Palace with her friend just behind her, she sensed that something was wrong. The bustle of preparations had completely gone and there were raised voices coming from the Grand Hall.

"Oh, my glittering whiskers!" murmured the White Cat. "Whatever has happened?"

Together they hurried through to the Grand Hall and her friend gasped. "Oh, my shimmering tail!"

He pointed ahead of him to where a glass case set high on a golden stool stood empty.

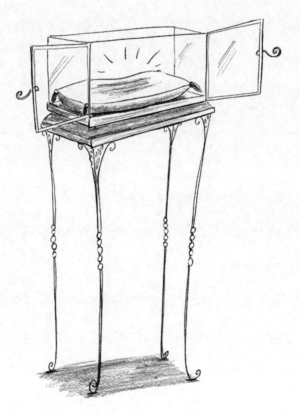

"What is it, Cat?" Jade asked in scarcely more than a whisper.

"It's the Silver Flute," he exclaimed. "It's missing!"

Tricked!

Everyone in the Grand Hall was staring at the empty glass case.

"That's where the flute should be," the White Cat said, wringing his tail between his paws. "It's been stolen like everything else! Oh, my shining eyes, Jade! What are we going to do?"

Jade's mind was racing. Why were things going missing – and why *these* items in particular? *Maybe there's a connection between them*, she thought. But what could it be? A silver baby's spoon, a ruby ring, a sparkling tiara, a silver flute...

As she pictured them all in her head, an idea popped into her mind.

"White Cat! Are all the things that have disappeared made of silver?"

The White Cat frowned and then nodded. "Yes, why?"

"Well, maybe the person who's stealing

wants them *because* they are silver…"
Jade broke off as she realised something.
"My scarf!" she gasped. "I gave it to that
lady – it was silver too!"

The White Cat stared at Jade. "Describe
her to me."

"I was more concerned with looking
out for you so I wasn't paying her much
attention, but let me see." Jade closed her
eyes to picture the lady better. "She was

tall and thin and had very good posture.
She looked smart in a long, grey
skirt…"

"…and were her eyes jet black?"
interrupted the White Cat.
Jade opened her own
eyes and nodded,
feeling fear mounting
up inside her, but not
being sure why.

"It sounds like the Dark Witch,"
whispered the White Cat, ushering Jade
from the Grand Hall. "You must have
heard the story of *Beauty and the Beast*?"

"The Dark Witch?" Jade gasped. "The

one who put a curse on the Prince? But she told me to meet her here! Just outside the palace walls."

"Then that's exactly where we'll go!" exclaimed the White Cat.

"She's not here," said the White Cat as soon as they got outside. "And it's much more than an hour since I met you. I think we can safely say she tricked you, Jade."

"But why?" asked Jade. "Why would she be collecting silver things? What could she possibly want them for?"

"That's what we need to find out," replied the White Cat. "But most importantly we need to get the Silver Flute back in time for the ceremony. We must go to the Dark Witch's castle!"

Jade's heart was pounding as she stepped into the circle that the White Cat was drawing on the ground with his tail. Immediately silver sparkles appeared, spinning around them and lifting them up.

In a matter of moments, the White Cat's magic had set them down in a garden full of dead flowers, surrounded by a withered brown hedge.

"Is this where she lives?" Jade asked quietly.

The White Cat nodded towards a tall grey tower. "*That's* where she lives."

Then he narrowed his eyes. "Can you hear muttering?"

Jade listened hard. It was the same voice that had told her about her scarf having a thread loose, only now it was low and gloating.

"Come on, we can spy on her," said the White Cat, tiptoeing towards the hedge.

Through their peepholes, Jade and the White Cat looked at an open courtyard of dark cobblestones. In the middle stood a large squat cauldron that bubbled with silver liquid. A tiny spoon bobbed up and down on the top.

"That's baby Pearl's!" whispered the

White Cat sorrowfully.

Hanging over the sludgy mixture, stirring it energetically was the lady that Jade had met earlier. Only now she wasn't dressed in her simple grey clothes. She was wearing a pointed hat – it was the Dark Witch!

"Very good, very good… the magic must be working by now," she muttered smugly. Then her tone changed to a raucous chant.

"*Beauty's Prince indeed!*
Silver, silver speed!
Do your magic deed!"

The Dark Witch bent down to the ground before raising something up and holding it over the cauldron so that it fluttered in the billowing steam. Jade stifled a gasp when she realised it was the silver scarf.

"*Silver from above*
Flutters like a dove.

Prince, fall out of love!"

The Dark Witch let the scarf drop into the seething cauldron.

"This is what will be –
No more He and She!
The Prince will now love ME!"

A high-pitched cackle of glee filled the air and Jade flinched with shock, leaning closer to the White Cat. "She's concocting a spell to make the Prince fall out of love with Beauty and *in* love with *her*?" she gasped.

"It certainly looks that way," the White

Cat nodded grimly. Then he and Jade turned to each other in horror because they saw the Dark Witch was holding something else above the cauldron. The Silver Flute!

"This will make sure that the spell definitely works," she cried, uncurling her fingers. "Here comes the purest silver." She held the flute high and muttered, "Magic, finish thy work."

The Bubbling Cauldron

Before she even had time to think, Jade yelled, "Stop!"

Rushing out from the hedge into the open courtyard, she found herself face to face with the Dark Witch. She stood frozen like a statue staring at Jade, the

flute still in her hand.

"Who are you and what do you want? How DARE you come to my castle uninvited!"

She lowered the flute and took a step forward, peering at Jade through the steam from the cauldron. Then a look of recognition came over her face and her lip curled. "Ah, so it's you. I never had any intention of giving your scarf back, you silly little girl, and there's no point in telling me to stop. It's too late for that." She pointed a long white finger towards the cauldron. "Your scarf is in there! And if you don't make yourself scarce, you'll follow it. Now go on, disappear, I'm busy."

The Dark Witch turned back to the cauldron, holding the flute high again.

"No, please stop!" repeated Jade, her heart banging against her ribs. "You see, I couldn't help hearing your spell just now…"

Jade was frantically racking her brain for what to say next. Any second now the flute would be turned into melted silver sludge. She swallowed and rushed on, "…the thing is, you mustn't put the flute in there because… because…"

"…because the spell won't work!" A voice behind her finished off the sentence.

Jade and the Dark Witch both turned to see the White Cat standing there as though it was the most natural thing in the world to show up without warning at someone else's castle.

The Dark Witch spoke in a low threatening tone. "I'm getting fed up with all these interruptions! You're just a girl," she said turning to Jade. "And you're just a moggy!" She eyed the White Cat out of the corner of her eye. "Why should you know anything about *my* spell? Take this silly girl with you and get back to where you came from!"

"Ah, now that's just the point," said the White Cat.

Jade couldn't help admiring the way he sounded so confident, but what on earth was he about to say?

"You see we have just come from the

castle of Beauty and
the Prince."

The Dark Witch had
turned back to her
cauldron, but she swung around again
at those words. "Yes?" Her coal black
eyes looked greedy to hear more.

The White Cat threw the tiniest of glances
at Jade as if to say *help me out here.*

Jade thought quickly. She had to keep
the Dark Witch's attention. "Yes, we
were… just passing their castle when we
saw Beauty in the garden."

"Looking so very sad…" continued the
White Cat.

And in a flash, the perfect story popped into Jade's head. "Beauty was crying and mumbling to herself…" she went on.

The Dark Witch's eyebrows twitched and her eyes began to gleam. "Was she indeed?"

"Yes, we heard her say that the Prince might be falling out of love with her. She seemed in a terrible state, talking to herself about how worried she was, in case it meant he was falling *in* love with someone else."

A smug look came over the Dark Witch's face. "Go on." She was staring into the distance with a dreamy look on her face.

Jade exchanged the most fleeting of glances with the White Cat. This was going to be the tricky bit. "So… you see, your spell is already working. There's no need to add any more silver to the mixture. Or it might be *too* strong."

The Dark Witch's dreamy look was replaced by a suspicious one. "What?"

Jade hurried on, trying to sound more confident than she felt. "If there's too much silver there's a risk that the Prince might fall in love with more than one person."

The bubbling cauldron seemed very loud as Jade held her breath. But a second later the silence was shockingly broken.

"Poppycock!" spat the Dark Witch.
"What do *you* know about magic?" The
hand that held the flute was trembling
with fury.

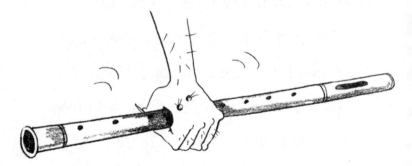

Jade gulped. "I've learnt magic from
the White Cat!" she quickly said, looking
apologetically at her friend because now
it was up to him to think of something.

The White Cat crossed one leg over the other casually at the ankles and stroked his whiskers as though he wasn't really bothered what the Dark Witch did. "All I know is that it would be much safer to add just a few more drops of silver rather than a whole flute," he said lightly.

The Dark Witch seemed to deflate at those words. "And where am I supposed to get these *few drops* from exactly?" she asked, a note of uncertainty in her voice.

"From me!" replied the White Cat. "Watch carefully."

Jade didn't know what her friend was going to do, but she didn't have to wait long. Suddenly, his whiskers began to twitch and a moment later they started to glow. The glow turned to a bright glitter and silver sparks began to fly around him. He jumped into the air, criss-crossing his ankles and landed gracefully in first position. But as he landed something extraordinary happened.

Jade couldn't believe her eyes. Some of the sparkles splashed into the cauldron.

The Dark Witch still looked suspicious.

 Jade and the Silver Flute

"You may be right, but you might not be." Her eyes narrowed. "I'm sure I know more about magic than you!" And she lifted the flute.

Jade's stomach turned to ice. "But what if it *is* true? You'll be ruining the spell. Wasting all the silver you have collected. Don't do it!"

The Dark Witch seemed caught up with doubt and the flute hovered above the slimy concoction.

Jade searched her mind urgently for the right thing to say. "We can prove it!" she blurted out. But as soon as the words were out of her mouth, she wished them back in. She'd just said the first thing that had come into her head. Jade turned helplessly to the White Cat.

"I will magic us all to Beauty and the Prince's castle," he said calmly.

There was another silence while Jade crossed her fingers behind her back. Then the Dark Witch seemed to leap into action. "I'm not going anywhere with *you two*!" she declared stoutly. "I shall go on my own!"

From out of nowhere a wand flew into her hand and, in a flash, she disappeared.

Beauty and the Prince

"There's no time to lose!" said the White Cat the moment he and Jade found themselves alone. "She's still got the Silver Flute. We need to get to Beauty and the Prince's castle immediately."

"But then what?" Jade said despairingly.

"We'll think of something," said the White Cat, swishing his tail in a circle.

Jade's mind was racing as she jumped into the sparkly ring.

The White Cat's magic set them down just outside Beauty and the Prince's garden and soon they spotted the Dark Witch peering through the hedge. She didn't notice Jade and the White Cat's arrival.

"There's Beauty!" said Jade in a tremulous whisper, as she peeped through another part of the hedge a little distance

away. "She's even more beautiful than I thought she'd be."

"And there's the Prince," the White Cat pointed out. "He loves watching Beauty dancing."

"I recognise that dance she's doing," said Jade. "It's the one I was performing at my audition just before I was brought to Enchantia. Only Beauty's dancing it about ten times more gracefully and smoothly than I could," she sighed.

As the dance finished, Beauty's soft lilting voice rang out. "Let us go inside and watch the sunset from the balcony!" She linked her arm through the Prince's and they started to walk towards the castle smiling at each other.

At the mention of sunset Jade was instantly jolted out of her trance. Her eyes shot to the reddening sky and her heart missed a beat as she realised with a sinking feeling that time was running out. Once the sun had set it would be too late for the First Fairy's dance. She turned to the White Cat and saw her own fear reflected in his eyes.

"Well, she didn't exactly look sad to me!" the Dark Witch suddenly called out. She had rounded on Jade and the White Cat and was standing over them, dark and furious with the flute in one hand, her wand in the other. "And as for the

Prince! He's not falling out of love. What wicked lies you've been spinning! I'm going back to my castle. This flute is going in the cauldron along with any other silver I can lay my hands on. And I

don't want to see you two again. *Ever*!
Do you *understand*?"

The Dark Witch swiped her wand
through the air in fury as she prepared to
return to her castle.

Jade knew this was her last chance.
"No, you still don't understand!" she
cried passionately. "The dance that
Beauty was doing was to try and stop the
Prince falling out of love with her. He
loves watching her dance. It's one of his
favourite things. The reason she looked so
happy then was because she thought that
the dance was working – that it was
stopping him from falling *out* of love

with her." Jade waited for the words to sink in.

The Dark Witch frowned deeply. Her neck jutted forwards. Then her feet shuffled slightly as she began muttering, "So what are you saying? That the Prince loves dancing so much that I will have to learn to dance to keep him in love with me, once I have lured him away? Yes, yes, you're right. I do need to learn to dance. I *have* to learn to dance!"

The moment had come. Jade took a deep breath.

"I can teach you the dance," she said casually.

Jade wasn't expecting what came next.

The Dark Witch suddenly pointed her wand at Jade like a sword. "Do it!" she commanded. "Follow me back to my castle, and teach me the wretched dance!" The wand swiped through the air again and in an instant she was gone.

Jade turned slowly to her friend. He laid a paw on her arm and spoke gently. "Will you be able to teach her the dance or were you just saying that?"

Jade nodded quickly. "I'm going to try my very hardest to dance just as smoothly and serenely as Beauty did just now."

"Quite so!" said the White Cat, his eyes starting to twinkle. "I'll keep on my toes. I might be able to grab the flute while you're dancing. Come on, let's get back quickly."

Jade glanced at the sinking sun and felt another tremor of fear as she stepped into the White Cat's circle.

"You two took your time!" snapped the Dark Witch once Jade and the White Cat were set down in her courtyard.

Jade noticed with relief that the Silver Flute was propped up against a dead shrub near the bubbling cauldron. She took a few steps away, thinking that the White Cat might be able to snatch the flute when they danced. Then she turned to the witch. "Why don't I teach you over here? It's a better surface."

The Dark Witch stayed put. "There's nothing wrong with this surface!" She tapped it with her wand. "Get on with it, girl! Show me the first bit."

A picture of Beauty dancing filled Jade's head as she raised her arms to fifth position and extended her leg in a *developpé*. It would have felt wonderful if only she

hadn't been so anxious about the darkening sky. She couldn't lose herself in the dance with her mind so full of fear. Yet she knew she must. Time was running out.

With a great effort of will Jade made herself close her eyes so she could concentrate better. When she opened them a few seconds later she saw the Dark Witch swaying slightly, a gentler expression than usual hovering around the hard features of her face. Jade stole a subtle glance at the White Cat and felt a ray of hope. He was definitely up to something. His eyes were fixed on the cauldron and glittering strongly.

Jade made herself stay focused. If she could just keep the Dark Witch distracted a moment longer…

She extended her right arm to the fingertips and tipped her head as she pointed her left foot behind her as smoothly as she could. The Dark Witch tipped her own head to the side and tried to imitate Jade's position.

Then suddenly, out of nowhere came a deafening explosion.

Jade jumped with shock. The cauldron had tipped over, its contents spilling out and starting to solidify into an iron-grey mulch. Silver-black steam billowed all around as a screech from the Dark Witch filled the air.

The Ceremony

"Keep back!" yelled the White Cat.

Jade did as she was told. But the Dark Witch was stuck. She had been standing so close to the cauldron that she couldn't help stepping in the slimy mulch. Now she was slipping and sliding around, her

arms turning like windmills as she tried
to stay on her feet. Jade found herself
stifling a giggle, even though the situation
was so serious.

"Come on! I've got the flute!" the
White Cat called urgently above the
high-pitched screams of the skidding
witch and the deep gurgle of the
darkening sludge.

But Jade had spotted the tiny spoon,
still undamaged, floating in the spillage.
She rushed towards it.

"No! There's no time!" cried the White
Cat.

Jade couldn't help herself. Reaching
down, she grabbed the spoon then
jumped back just before a racing
streamlet of silver reached her toes.
Clutching the spoon, she dashed over

to the White Cat who was firmly holding

the Silver Flute. Quick as a flash, he

swished his tail rapidly and a ring of

sparks flew around them like electricity.

"Phew, we made it!" gasped Jade as they landed just outside the Royal Palace.

"Our job isn't done yet, though," cried the White Cat. "Look!"

Jade's stomach yo-yoed as she noticed the sun – a soft red ball on the horizon, about to sink out of sight.

Together they raced inside the Palace and through to the Grand Hall. Serious faces greeted them, but they didn't waver for a second and rushed over to the golden stool with the glass case. Gently, the White Cat opened the door and placed the

flute upon the gold and red cushion. And
immediately the First Fairy rose on to
pointe.

There was the briefest moment of
stunned silence, then a sweet magical
melody rang out and filled the air. The

First Fairy fluttered on her pointes before performing a series of light springs from one foot to the other, her hands and arms weaving patterns in the air.

Looking round Jade saw only smiles now, and the biggest smile was on the face of her clever friend the White Cat. They'd been through such an adventure together. Jade impulsively reached for his paw and they exchanged a quick look before they were drawn like magnets back to the First Fairy's dance.

Her movements seemed to follow the shape of the tune as it trilled and rippled up and down. Jade clasped her hands together and watched in awe until the very last note melted away. Then everyone burst into applause and the First Fairy ran with the lightest footsteps to where Jade and the White Cat were standing.

"Thank you both!" she whispered as she planted a fluttery kiss on each of their cheeks.

After that everyone wanted to congratulate them and to hear the story of how they'd managed to recover the Silver Flute from the clutches of the evil Dark Witch. There were looks of dismay when

the people heard that Jade had lost her
silver scarf. But it was an especially
wonderful moment when King Tristan
and Queen Isabella came over.

"We thank you from the bottom of our

hearts," said the Queen.

King Tristan nodded. "You are a brave pair! What could have happened without our precious flute doesn't bear thinking about."

Then the best moment of all came when Jade handed the silver spoon to Cinderella, who promptly burst into tears of joy.

"I can't believe you managed to retrieve this precious spoon for Pearl!" she said, her eyes sparkling with the tears. "Especially as you were unable to save your own scarf. I don't care about my napkin ring, but this spoon is very dear to my heart. Thank you so much, Jade. Wait two seconds."

With that Cinderella positively flew across the hall and returned with a beautiful silver scarf that she held out to her. "For you, as a special thank you."

Jade felt as though she could burst with happiness. The scarf was almost exactly the same as the one that Madame Za-Za

had lent her, just a bit glossier. "Thank you, Cinderella."

The White Cat winked at Jade. "What a perfect gift!"

There was lots of dancing to live music, though the Silver Flute never played again.

"It only ever plays for the First Fairy just once a year," the White Cat explained.

Jade and her friend joined in another dance and then sat down to talk through everything that had happened.

"The way you made the cauldron tip over was amazing," Jade congratulated her friend. "Didn't the Dark Witch look funny skating about like that!"

"But you and your dancing – that was brilliant too." The White Cat chuckled then looked thoughtful. "I must admit, magicking the silver sparks from my whiskers was a bit of an experiment! I knew I had the magical power to do it, but it's never actually been put to the test before."

Jade clapped her hands delightedly. "Good timing, White Cat!"

"Well, thank you!" said the White Cat, his eyes twinkling merrily. "And talking of timing…" He looked down.

Jade followed his gaze. Her shoes were glowing brightly, ready to take her back to the real world.

"Well goodbye, White Cat. See you again!" said Jade.

"Of course!" Jade's friend reached
down and picked something off the floor.
"Oh, my shining eyes! This scarf is so
light you didn't even notice you'd
accidentally let it fall!"

Jade laughed and thanked him as her
feet tingled and rainbow colours began to
swirl around her faster and faster.

Back at the Studio

As Jade's feet touched the ground, she looked around her in confusion for a moment. She was back in the small studio, waiting for Madame Za-Za to return and, as usual, no time had passed in the real world while she'd been in

Enchantia. She was still clutching the scarf that Cinderella had given her and she threw it lightly in the air, smiling as it fluttered down. Madame Za-Za had hoped the scarf might help her to dance more expressively. So Jade rose on to demi-pointe and closed her eyes for a second.

Immediately her mind was flooded with the memory of Beauty dancing in her garden. And when she opened her eyes again, a feeling of serenity took over her body. She found herself dancing with more grace and smoothness than ever before, from her feet to the top of her head and down to the tips of her fingers.

As she held the final pose, she was startled by the sound of clapping and looked round to see Madame Za-Za standing by the door.

"I didn't realise you'd come back in," Jade said quietly.

"I have been here for some time," Madame Za-Za smiled, "but you were so lost in your dance that you didn't even notice me." Coming forward, she took Jade's hands in her own. "And *I, too*, was lost in the dance. You really drew me in which is what true ballet is all about. Well done indeed!"

Jade could hardly contain her happiness. It felt so wonderful to receive such praise. She handed Madame Za-Za the scarf. "I couldn't have done it without you – or without this for that matter!"

Madame Za-Za nodded. "I thought it might help, my dear." Then a puzzled look came over her face. "I must be imagining it, but the scarf looks somehow even silkier and smoother than it did before. How extraordinary!"

"Doesn't it," agreed Jade.

As she turned to leave the studio she hid a smile and her head filled with the sound of a magical melody played on a very special Silver Flute.

Développé

Be as beautiful as Beauty from Beauty and the Beast as you practise the 'unfolding step' in her elegant dance.

1.
Start with your feet in fifth position. Place your left hand on the barre (or the back of a chair) and hold your right arm in preparatory position.

2.
Gently open your lower right arm sideways starting with your hand whilst watching your fingertips. Bring your arm back through preparatory position.

3.
As you lift your right leg, your toe will come up in front of your left leg to your knee. Raise your right arm to first position.

4.
As your toe reaches your knee, unfold your right leg, keeping your knee out, and open your arm to second position.

5.
Smoothly extend and straighten your right leg as high as you can. Hold your leg still then slowly lower it into fifth position.

Magic Ballerina

Jade and the Carnival

It's carnival time! But not everyone is enjoying the dancing. Why is Leonardo the toymaker so sad?

Read on for a sneak preview of Jade's next adventure...

As soon as Jade's feet touched the ground, she felt excitement mounting inside her. It looked as though she'd stepped right into the middle of a wonderful carnival in Enchantia. What a coincidence when she'd only just been practising for her own local music and dance festival! This one was much bigger and grander though.

Jade was standing in a wide avenue full of brightly coloured stalls. The soldiers from the *Nutcracker* ballet were marching down the street playing trumpets and drums and there were people lining the avenue, clapping as they passed. Behind them came a group of clog dancers.

Laughter, music and cheering filled the air. And that wasn't all. Where was that delicious toffee-apple smell coming from? Jade followed her nose to try and track it down, but couldn't help stopping every so often to see what lovely trinkets, jewels and accessories the stalls held. Everyone was smiley and happy, except one person just ahead who looked very downcast. He was wearing a checked shirt and a leather waistcoat, dark coloured trousers that came just below the knee and a spotty scarf tied loosely around his neck.

I wonder what's making him so sad, thought Jade. Her hand suddenly flew to her mouth as she'd realised who was standing beside the dejected-looking man. It was her old friend, the White Cat. In her excitement at the magnificent carnival, she'd completely forgotten that the White Cat usually came to greet her when she arrived in Enchantia.

"White Cat! Hello!" she called, threading her way through the crowd.

He looked up and smiled. "Jade! I was expecting you!" The White Cat hugged her then introduced her to his unhappy friend. "This is Leonardo, the toymaker."

"Hello, Leonardo," Jade smiled, reaching out to shake his hand.

"Hello," Leonardo smiled gently, but he still looked so sad. Jade looked to the White Cat expectantly.

"Leonardo's precious puppet Peter has been stolen and put under someone else's spell," the White Cat explained.

Jade gasped. "Do you mean... Peter, the clown from the ballet *Petrouchka*?" she asked.

Leonardo nodded forlornly and through Jade's head flashed a series of pictures of the three puppets from the ballet – the Saracen with his jewelled turban and sword, the ballerina with her porcelain face and round blue eyes, and Petrouchka, the clown – Peter for short – with his baggy trousers and friendly smile.

"Peter has been helping me in my shop ever since I first made him," explained Leonardo in a thin voice. "And I miss him terribly. He's like a son to me because, although he looks like an ordinary puppet, he has a heart and can feel things." Leonardo's head dropped. "I can't bear to lose him like this."

To be continued...

The Story of Beauty and the Beast

Beauty lived with her two older sisters and her father, Claude. One day, Claude had to go on a long journey and he promised to bring back a present for each of his daughters.

"*I* want a lovely new dress," said the oldest girl.

"*I* want a pretty necklace," said her sister.

But Beauty smiled at her father. "Just bring me a red rose," she laughed as she kissed him goodbye.

On his way home Claude was caught in a terrible storm, but through the pouring rain he saw a castle with candlelight glowing at the windows. *Perhaps I can shelter there,* he thought.

He was surprised to find the castle's door standing open. "Hello," he called, but nobody answered. In the great hall he found a table laden with delicious food. He was hungry so he sat down and ate until he was full. Then he started to feel sleepy so he went upstairs, found a bed and fell asleep at once.

The next morning, as he was leaving he noticed a rose bush in the garden. *I'll take a flower home for Beauty,* he thought. But as he bent to pick a rose he heard a terrifying roar and an ugly beast leapt from behind the bush.

"How dare you steal my roses!" it growled. "For that I will keep you a prisoner in my castle for ever."

"But I only wanted one rose to give to my

daughter," explained Claude.

"If she likes roses so much she can be a prisoner here instead of you," snarled the Beast. Claude pleaded with him but the Beast refused to change his mind.

Beauty was very brave. When she heard the horrible news she agreed to go to the castle. But she didn't feel so brave when she met the Beast. He was dressed in fine clothes, but he had big claws, and sharp teeth and spoke in an angry growl.

What Beauty didn't know was that the Beast was really an enchanted Prince. The Dark Witch had put a horrid spell on him that could only be broken if somebody fell in love with him.

Beauty thought the Beast would make her live in the dungeon, but instead he gave her the prettiest bedroom in the castle. In the daytime she explored the garden, and in the evenings she sat by the huge fire and read books that the Beast had found for her. She often saw the Beast watching her but he never came to say hello. She thought  he was unfriendly, but really he was very shy.

Then one evening he came to sit with her by the fire. They started talking and Beauty realised the Beast wasn't scary, he was good and kind. After that they spent every day together.

"Do you like living here?" the Beast asked Beauty one day as they were having a picnic.

"Oh yes," she said, "now that we are friends. But sometimes I miss my family."

The next day the Beast gave Beauty a present. It was a magic silver mirror and when she looked into it she could see her family. "Oh, thank you," she cried and gave the Beast a hug.

Time passed happily until one day the Beast

found Beauty looking in the magic mirror and crying. Her father was very poorly and she wanted to visit him. The Beast was afraid that if she went home she wouldn't come back. But he hated to see her sad so he agreed. "But promise me you will return in seven days," he said and Beauty promised.

When she got home Beauty discovered that her father was ill because he was so worried about her. She sat by his bed and told him stories about her life at the castle, and how kind the Beast was. Now Claude knew that she was happy he slowly started to get better. But Beauty was so busy looking after

him she didn't realise that seven days had passed
and she had broken her promise to the Beast.

Looking in her magic mirror she saw him sitting
by the fire holding a red rose. He looked very thin
and very miserable. "Come back!
Come back to me!" he was
pleading. Beauty could
see that his heart was
breaking and realised that she
missed him. She hurriedly kissed her family
goodbye and rushed back to the castle.

"I'm sorry I stayed away so long," she cried
running to the Beast and throwing her arms around
him.

"My darling, Beauty," he said, "I missed you so
much. Will you marry me?"

"Of course I will," Beauty laughed, wiping away
her tears. At that moment a cloud of silver sparkles
rose up around the Beast and when the shimmering

cloud cleared he was no longer a Beast – the spell
had been broken and he was once more the
handsome Prince Valentino. "I love you," he told
Beauty.

"I love you, too," she replied.

They lived happily ever after.

Meet other girls in Enchantia over the page...

Hello, I'm Delphie. I wasn't sure why Madame Za-Za gave me a dusty pair of red ballet shoes until they started to glow and whisked me away to Enchantia! Sugar (also known as the Sugar Plum Fairy) befriended me there and we've had lots of magic times trying to outwit King Rat and spoil his evil plans. Together we've saved enchanted guests at a masked ball, broken wicked spells and ensured the Queen's birthday show was perfect!

Hair colour: Brown

Eye colour: Blue

Likes: practising ballet excercises, Enchantia

Dislikes: King Rat

Favourite ballet: The Nutcracker

Best friend in Enchantia: Sugar

Read all my Magic Ballerina adventures…

Hi, I'm Rosa. I've always loved dancing! Madame Za-Za tells me to slow down and concentrate on what I'm doing, but dancing is just so exciting. Delphie gave me the precious red ballet shoes and, before I knew it, I was in Enchantia meeting all the ballet characters. Nutmeg (Sugar's sister) and I have been on lots of adventures: rescuing an enchanted princess, finding stolen treasure and thwarting the Wicked Fairy at every turn.

Hair colour: Blonde

Eye colour: Blue

Likes: Olivia my best friend, making my mum happy

Dislikes: Making mistakes or losing my temper

Favourite ballet: Swan Lake

Best friend in Enchantia: Nutmeg

Read all my Magic Ballerina adventures…

Hi, my name's Holly and I love ballet more than anything. Dancing makes me think of my mum because she's a professional dancer. I love the emotions and stories in ballet, sometimes I get so carried away I forget where I am! Luckily I'm always in the best places: dancing at Madame Za-Za's or in Enchantia! The White Cat and I have done so much there: protecting Cinderella from an evil magician, reuniting Beauty and the Beast, and even making things right in the Land of Sweets!

Hair colour: Dark brown

Eye colour: Green

Likes: Expressing myself through dancing

Dislikes: Feeling left out

Favourite ballet: Sleeping Beauty (particularly the Rose Adagio dance)

Best friend in Enchantia: The White Cat

Read all my Magic Ballerina adventures...

15 Magic Ballerina — Holly and the Dancing Cat — Darcey Bussell

14 Magic Ballerina — Holly and the Silver Unicorn — Darcey Bussell

15 Magic Ballerina — Holly and the Magic Tiara — Darcey Bussell

16 Magic Ballerina — Holly and the Rose Garden — Darcey Bussell

17 Magic Ballerina — Holly and the Ice Palace — Darcey Bussell

18 Magic Ballerina — Holly and the Land of Sweets — Darcey Bussell

The White Cat's

Magic Ballerina Quiz

Think you know all there is to know about
the land of Enchantia and ballet?
Well why not test your knowledge with the
White Cat's Magic Ballerina quiz!
See how many questions you can get right
and become a ballet star.

(Check your answers on page 125)

1. What colour are the magic ballet shoes that can take you to Enchantia?

2. What is the name of Jade's ballet teacher?

3. Who is stealing silver objects in *Jade and the Silver Flute*?

4. What is the famous ballet about swans called?

5. Who builds a fun fair in *Jade and the Enchanted Wood*?

6. What colour are the White Cat's eyes?

7. What type of dancing other than ballet does Jade like?

8. With Jade's help, who undoes the Wicked Fairy's spell in *Jade and the Surprise Party*?

9. Where do the mouse guards live?

10. What is first position with your feet in ballet?

ANSWERS:

1. *red* 2. *Madame Za-Za* 3. *Dark Witch* 4. *Swan Lake* 5. *King Rat* 6. *green* 7. *street-dancing* 8. *Lila the Lilac Fairy* 9. *King Rat's castle* 10. *Turn your toes out to the sides with your heels touching.*

Darcey Bussell

Buy more great Magic Ballerina books direct from
HarperCollins at 10% off recommended retail price.
FREE postage and packing in the UK.

All priced at £3.99

To purchase by Visa/Mastercard/Maestro simply call
08707871724 or fax on **08707871725**

To pay by cheque, send a copy of this form with a cheque made payable to
'HarperCollins Publishers' to: Mail Order Dept. (Ref: BOB4),
HarperCollins Publishers, Westerhill Road, Bishopbriggs, G64 2QT,
making sure to include your full name, postal address and phone number.

From time to time HarperCollins may wish to use your personal data
to send you details of other HarperCollins publications and offers.
If you wish to receive information on other HarperCollins publications
and offers please tick this box ☐

Do not send cash or currency. Prices correct at time of press.
Prices and availability are subject to change without notice.
Delivery overseas and to Ireland incurs a £2 per book postage and packing charge.

Magic Ballerina

Darcey Bussell

Buy more great Magic Ballerina books direct from
HarperCollins at 10% off recommended retail price.
FREE postage and packing in the UK.

All priced at £3.99

To purchase by Visa/Mastercard/Maestro simply call
08707871724 or fax on **08707871725**

To pay by cheque, send a copy of this form with a cheque made payable to
'HarperCollins Publishers' to: Mail Order Dept. (Ref: BOB4),
HarperCollins Publishers, Westerhill Road, Bishopbriggs, G64 2QT,
making sure to include your full name, postal address and phone number.

From time to time HarperCollins may wish to use your personal data
to send you details of other HarperCollins publications and offers.
If you wish to receive information on other HarperCollins publications
and offers please tick this box ☐

Do not send cash or currency. Prices correct at time of press.
Prices and availability are subject to change without notice.
Delivery overseas and to Ireland incurs a £2 per book postage and packing charge.

Darcey Bussell

Buy more great Magic Ballerina books direct from
HarperCollins at **10%** off recommended retail price.
FREE postage and packing in the UK.

All priced at £3.99

To purchase by Visa/Mastercard/Maestro simply call
08707871724 or fax on **08707871725**

To pay by cheque, send a copy of this form with a cheque made payable to
'HarperCollins Publishers' to: Mail Order Dept. (Ref: BOB4),
HarperCollins Publishers, Westerhill Road, Bishopbriggs, G64 2QT,
making sure to include your full name, postal address and phone number.

From time to time HarperCollins may wish to use your personal data
to send you details of other HarperCollins publications and offers.
If you wish to receive information on other HarperCollins publications
and offers please tick this box ☐

Do not send cash or currency. Prices correct at time of press.
Prices and availability are subject to change without notice.
Delivery overseas and to Ireland incurs a £2 per book postage and packing charge.